W9-BTC-712

The Fabulous Four Skunks

David Fair   Illustrated by Bruce Koscielniak

Houghton Mifflin Company
Boston New York 1996

For information about this and other Houghton Mifflin
trade and reference books and multimedia products,
visit The Bookstore at Houghton Mifflin on the World Wide
Web at (http://www.hmco.com/trade/).

Library of Congress Cataloging-in-Publication Data

Fair, David.
  The fabulous four skunks / David Fair : illustrated by Bruce
Koscielniak.
     p. cm.
  Summary: When four skunks who form a rock and roll band play at
the teen center, they provide a clothespin for everyone who attends
the performance.
  ISBN 0-395-73572-6 (hardcover)
  [1. Skunks—Fiction.   2. Rock music—Fiction.   3. Bands (Music)—
Fiction.]   I. Koscielniak, Bruce, ill.   II. Title.
PZ7.F144Fab   1996
[E]—dc20   95-23383   CIP   AC

Printed in Singapore

TWP 10 9 8 7 6 5 4 3 2 1

For Susan and Robinson —D.F.

Four skunks formed a rock and roll band. Stenchy played drums, Reeky played bass, Smelly played guitar, and Stinky sang.

They practiced in Stenchy's basement, and Stinky wrote
lots of songs for them to play.

"We've got to think of a name for our band," said Stinky.
So they all wrote down suggestions and finally settled on
The Four Skunks.

One night during practice, Stenchy's mom brought down some snacks. She winked at Stenchy and gave Smelly a pat on the back. "You sound good enough to play at the teen center," she said.

The next day, Smelly borrowed a tape recorder, and
The Four Skunks made a tape of their five best songs.

They mailed the tape to the manager of the teen center,
along with a letter that asked if they could have a job.

One week later they got a call from the manager. Stenchy was too nervous to talk, so she handed the phone to Stinky. The manager said he loved the tape, and asked Stinky if The Four Skunks could come to the teen center that weekend for an audition. "You bet!" shrieked Stinky.

There was so much to do. The four friends rehearsed for hours every day after school. Stenchy painted the name of the band on the front of her drum. Smelly and Reeky changed their guitar strings, and Stinky practiced bowing.

That weekend they loaded their equipment into Stenchy's dad's van and rode to the teen center.

As soon as they arrived, everyone left.

"Where did everybody go?" wondered Smelly.
"Golly, I don't know," answered Stinky. "I guess
they'll be right back. Let's set up our equipment."

They began tuning the guitars when they heard the
manager's voice from the back of the room. "You guys stink!"
he shouted.

"We're just tuning up," responded Smelly. "Wait til you hear
us play one of our songs."

Songs
For
Audition
1. Skunk Rock
2. Skunk Blues
3. Skunk Hop

Stenchy counted off the beat, and The Four Skunks began playing their first song. When they finished, they heard the manager's voice again. "You stink!" he yelled. "Get off the stage!"

"We're just beginners," admitted Smelly, "but lots of folks think we sound great."

"Come on, guys," muttered Stenchy. "I guess we don't get the job."

"Not so fast!" shouted the manager. "You get the job, all right. I just got an idea."

"But you said we stink," squeaked Stenchy.

"Never mind that," choked the manager. "Your music sounds great. I want you to play tomorrow night. It will be the greatest dance of the year. You just show up at seven, and I'll take care of everything."

"Okay!" said The Four Skunks. And they scurried home to practice.

The next night they returned to the teen center at seven sharp and saw a long line of excited kids waiting to get in.

A big sign over the door said, Appearing Tonight:
The Fabulous Four Skunks.

Stenchy, Reeky, Smelly, and Stinky followed the manager down a long hallway to a tiny dressing room.

"You go on in ten minutes," he said. "Don't worry about a thing."

They felt nervous but not worried. Stinky made a list
of the songs they planned to play, while Reeky and Smelly
tuned their guitars.

Stenchy forgot to bring in her drumsticks and ran out to the van to get them. Several of the kids fainted when she ran past. *This is exciting!* she thought. *We're famous already!*

Finally, it was showtime. The four friends scampered
on-stage and patiently waited for their introduction.

"Here is a band that should go far," joked the manager. "And the farther the better. Boys and girls, please welcome The Fabulous Four Skunks!"

The curtains parted, the spotlight beamed, and The Four Skunks nervously began to play.

After the first song everyone cheered. The audience loved them. "Blay somb more songs," screamed somebody.

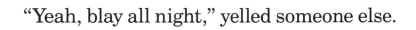
"Yeah, blay all night," yelled someone else.

"We lub you," chanted the audience. "We lub The Four Skunks!"